SLAVERY OF THE MIND

Slavery of the Mind

Discover what you can do and how to do it

Pusonnam Yiri

AFRICA CHRISTIAN TEXTBOOKS

2015

DEDICATION

To the ministry of reconciliation to God.

CONTENTS

ACKNOWLEDGEMENTS

I am grateful to God for blessing me with the grace to write this book. To Him be the glory.

I appreciate my lovely wife, Helen, and children for their love and support.

I thank my editors: Mr. Androcles H. Murray, Prof. & Mrs. Brown, Mr. Ishaku Bulus, Rev. Jerry Faruk and Dr Paul Todd for their contributions.

I am also grateful to my parents, ACTS management and board, Daveco, and all those who have contributed to this project in different ways.

I also appreciate my colleagues in ministry, brother and sisters.

INTRODUCTION

Everybody is a seed.

In Abuja, I once discussed with someone, who was worried about his situation. At night, a few hours after the discussion, he called and thanked me for the ideas I shared with him.

Moreover, during a live radio programme, in which I was invited as a guest, the text messages received during and after the programme, and a few calls pointed towards two basic questions of life, What can I do? and How can I do it? This book is an attempt to answer the questions; so that you would have knowledge that would enable you have victory over the bondage of frustration, into a purposeful and fruitful life in Jesus.

We are stewards of the potential in us. Dont let bitterness come out of sugar. No matter the errors you have committed in the past, there is good news. It is never too late to make it right.

I need to inform you that the character whose name was Peter in the first edition has been renamed to Nachau Turomale.

CHAPTER 1

"I will deal with you if I see you talking to Nina again," Kanem said angrily as he grasped Gange's shirt, after meeting him working alone on his father's farm.

"I don't like your attitude Kanem. Leave me alone if you know what is good for you," Gange fearfully replied.

"Stop me if you are a man. This is the last warning I am giving. I am the only man fit for her in this village!" Kanem challenged.

"A girl becomes fit for one man only after her marriage. I love Nina, and I don't think you or anybody can separate us," Gange responded attempting to be strong.

"No man talks to me like that," Kanem harshly said, as he slapped Gange hard.

Blood gushed out of Gange's nose. Gange could not retaliate, knowing full well the damage Kanem could cause him if the conflict escalated. He walked away struggling to control the bleeding with his shirt.

Feeling himself a conqueror, Kanem proudly rained insults on Gange as he watched him move away like a toothless bulldog.

Gange told his father what had happened when he got home. Later his father reported Kanem to the village elders.

Both the elders and many people of Moran village were worried about Kanem's behaviour. Many of them feared him, and wished him dead. His mother, a widow, failed to keep him under control. She often asked the elders for help in talking to her son.

Kanem was his parents' only surviving son. Two of his brothers had died of some illnesses a few months previously. All his efforts after his 'O' level education to be the best person in the village seemed to fall apart. He was an intelligent young man from a poor family, who believed that there was neither hope for him, nor anyone unconnected to wealth, to have an achievable dream. He was lost in a world where everything seemed meaningless to him.

His father had been a terror to the village. He had lived as a thief and a drunkard. Many people in the village saw the deaths of Kanem's father and brothers as punishment from God on the family.

Kanem grew up extremely bitter at his father. He refused to forgive his father for his careless attitude towards his family. His father had died without being reconciled with his son, because Kanem refused to see him on his sick bed, even after his father sent for him.

Many of the village people rejoiced in the death of Kanem's father and stigmatized the family as cursed. Hence, Kanem grew up without experiencing communal acceptance and love. The only way he knew he could pay the people in the village in the same coin, was to be a greater terror than his father had been.

Most of the young men from the village went to Lagos State in search of greener pastures. At the end of each year, they returned to the village for Christmas celebrations. It was always a moment for displaying their wealth, and harassing Kanem and other young men, who had not had the opportunity of working in Lagos.

Pamale was the only childhood friend that Kanem had who cared for him, and often wished he would one day join him in Lagos for work, so that he too could have a better lifestyle.

*

The elders of the village called an emergency meeting, and summoned Kanem and his mother to discuss his case with Gange. The elders could no longer tolerate Kanem's behaviour in the village. They knew that if drastic action was not taken, he would prey on more people. The District Head and all the elders of the village attended the meeting.

Kanem knew that his nemesis had caught up with him, when on arriving, he found the council of elders already seated.

Soon after the meeting began, the District Head announced Kanem's banishment from the village. He was given one week to prepare his belongings and leave the village, or face the collective wrath of the villagers.

The pronouncement shocked Kanem and his mother. In tears, his mother pleaded with the elders to have mercy on her son, but her pleas fell on deaf ears.

The crowd outside the meeting venue, who had earlier been waiting for the outcome of the meeting, applauded the elders' decision.

Kanem and his mother returned home in shame. His mother took some time to talk sense into him. Her tears were uncontrollable as she warned him of the further consequences awaiting him, if he refused to change his lifestyle.

That night, Kanem could hardly sleep. He spent much time thinking of what he could do to settle scores with his fellow-villagers for the embarrassment they had caused his mother and him.

As a way out, the idea of visiting Pamale in Lagos and securing a job flashed into his mind. He believed that once he secured a job and worked hard in Lagos, he could save some money and eventually become rich. With money in hand, he knew he could easily make his village people feel the pain of the sword of vengeance.

When he shared his decision with his mother, she quickly accepted the idea; but as a mother, she knew she would miss her only son whom she loved dearly, despite his reckless lifestyle. She feared that he would easily be killed in the city, if he didn't give up his lifestyle. She removed some money from her savings, and gave it to him to support his journey.

*

The next day, Kanem went to see Nina for an important discussion about their future.

On his way to the house, he suddenly ran into her, on her way home from the stream, carrying on her head a clay pot full of water.

"Nina," Kanem joyfully called, as he ran towards her.

Nina turned, looked at him, and ignoring him continued to move away.

"Nina, Nina," he desperately persisted to make her stop.

"Why are you disturbing me?" Nina rudely responded.

"I really want us to talk," Kanem said with a smile.

"I don't have time for you!" Nina reacted.

"Why are you talking like that? Have you forgotten the promises of love we shared?" Kanem asked.

"Love has no place between us anymore. I can no longer tolerate your reckless lifestyle and harassment of people because of me!"

"Life will have no meaning for me without you, Nina!" Kanem lamented.

"That is not my problem. Please, let me go!"

"Wherever I go, no matter what happens to me, I will not forget you!"

"It is better you forget me!" Nina emphasized, as she moved away from him.

His courage was broken, as he helplessly watched the love of his life disappear into thin air.

*

The thoughts of Nina held Kanem captive at night. He remembered the good old days when Nina told him how much she loved him and wished to have him as her husband in the future. He also thought of how he had also promised to protect their love with his life. All these had become a nightmare. He realized that life is full of mysteries, fragile in nature, and willing to give and take away its fragrance of happiness.

The pressure on him that night had subdued his courage. He cried bitterly on his bed, waking his mother with the sound of his weeping. The thought of her son's condition pierced her heart. She remembered how he was a source of joy to her before his love for worldly pleasure corrupted his heart. She picked her lantern and walked to his room, which was close to her own. On reaching there, she knocked at his door twice, but there was no positive reply.

She entered uninvited, put the lantern on the floor, and sat on the bed beside him. "Kanem, why are you crying?"

Kanem did not respond to her question. He only continued soaking his pillow with tears.

"Crying will not help you, my son. It will only make things worse."

"Everybody hates me, even Nina!" Kanem reacted angrily.

"But you don't have to blame them for their actions. Change your lifestyle if you want them to treat you well. You are the problem, not the people."

Kanem stood up quickly in anger. "It was not my fault, mother! I will deal with them for treating us like animals!"

"Don't make things worse for us, my son. Accepting your fault is the beginning of healing."

"I will not leave this village. It is also my village. I have equal rights just like everybody!" Kanem responded bitterly.

"These people would harm you if you try to be stubborn. You know quite well that they meant what they said. A proverb says that 'with a good approach, a young goat can suck a hyena's breast,'" the mother emphasized. With that, she stood up, and went to her room.

Kanem thought over what his mother had said, especially the proverb.

*

The rain was so heavy that it seemed as if the huts in the village would collapse. It was long since they had experienced such a heavy downpour.

Hope built in Kanem's mother's heart when she saw the rain the day her son was to leave the village. She thought that the rain would be a good reason to delay the expulsion until the next day, so that she could have more time with him. Suddenly, she heard a bang on the door. It was as if someone was breaking it. On opening the door, she saw two of the District Head's guards, waiting to escort Kanem out of the village.

Kanem and his mother were surprised to see the crowd, who despite the heavy rain, were singing mockery songs, and dancing over Kanem's banishment. Kanem noticed Nina amidst them, behaving restlessly, as if she was involved against her wish. It was like a dream to him, the worst day of his life.

Picking up his wet bag, which had been thrown on the ground by the guards, he slowly walked away in frustration into another life.

His mother was the only one crying. Other women insulted her and her late husband for their carelessness in training Kanem. Defencelessly, she walked away from the crowd to her hut. The thought of her husband flashed into her mind. She bitterly remembered how she tried without success to convince him to change his lifestyle and give sufficient time in training their children.

Kanem thought of vengeance, as he walked to the bus station wet and shivering because of the cold. On arriving there, he observed that nobody was interested in his presence. Some of the drivers of the buses insulted him. They refused to take him to the next town, 13 kilometres away, to enable him get a bus from there to Yola, the capital of Adamawa State, from where he would book a bus for his trip.

Kanem was forced to trek. On the way, he not only worried about himself, but also the sudden loneliness that would come upon his mother.

On reaching Yola, he went to the bus station, and booked a seat in a big 'luxurious bus.' He had no option, but to sleep at the station. It was a long night for him. He had spent much time thinking deeply about his new experiences.

The next morning, when it was time for the passengers to board the bus, Kanem also got on it. Holding his bag tightly he eagerly looked for the seat number on his receipt. Eventually, he found it. Sitting nervously he watched others board the bus and find their seats. Like them, he kept his bag right above the seat.

As the passengers were getting ready, suddenly, the driver entered the bus, and blew the horn repeatedly implying that all passengers should get ready for the journey.

As soon as the driver began to drive, a shout was heard from outside, urging him to stop. A passenger, who had been delayed because of a car with a flat tyre, wanted to board. His name was Nachau Turomale. He was 46 years old and an author who had written five books that were widely read. He believed that everything was meant to be utilized well. He always viewed his meeting with anybody as an opportunity to teach, and to learn new ideas about life.

Politely, Nachau apologized and explained to the conductor the reason for his lateness, as he entered the bus and moved towards his seat.

When he reached his seat, which was next to Kanem, he kept his bag close to Kanem's bag, and sat on the seat.

After praying silently for some minutes, he warmly greeted Kanem, but Kanem responded reluctantly because he knew he had to be careful with strangers.

"I am Nachau Turomale," the stranger introduced himself. Kanem once again looked cautiously at Nachau and wondered aloud about the hasty relationship. He asked the conductor to change his seat, but the conductor refused. He reluctantly told Nachau his name. They shook hands and Nachau smiled at him, imagining the dilemma in Kanem's mind towards his quick approach.

Soon after departure, Nachau became involved in a conversation with Kanem. "I have a book for you to read, if you wouldn't mind."

Kanem kept quiet without paying attention to Nachau.

"I am sure you will enjoy the book," Nachau persisted, ignoring Kanem's attitude.

"I have many things to think about. Please, don't disturb me!" Kanem remarked angrily.

"Yola to Lagos is a long journey. You need a friend, if you want to enjoy the trip."

Nachau's advice finally broke Kanem's isolation.

"How far is Lagos?" Kanem reluctantly asked.

"Almost twenty four hours journey," Nachau replied.

"You mean we will be on this bus for almost a day?"

"Something like that," Nachau replied. "Is this your first trip to Lagos?"

"Yes," Kanem answered shyly.

"Are you a business man or a student?" Nachau asked.

"I am going to look for a job," Kanem quickly replied.

"What type of job?"

"Any job that will give me money."

"Including stealing?" Nachau jokingly asked.

"No," Kanem smiled, as he replied.

"Must you go to Lagos to have such a job?"

"Many of my friends are working in Lagos."

"What kind of job do you hope to secure?"

"A house boy job."

"You are leaving Yola for Lagos only for a house boy job?" Nachau asked in surprise.

"All my friends in Lagos are house boys, and they are making some money from doing that."

"It seems like you love money," Nachau jokingly asked.

"Everybody loves money," Kanem quickly replied.

"What do you think is the purpose of life?"

"To make money, and live in comfort," Kanem confidently answered.

"Is this the reason why God created us?"

"Could there be any better reason than that?" Kanem anxiously asked.

"There is a reason that is more important than money."

"Are you sure?"

"Yes, I am very sure."

"What is that?"

"There are many different purposes, but there is only one major purpose. It should be the goal of everything you think, say and do, whether you are rich or poor, small or big, healthy or sick. If it is not the goal, then you are missing your purpose on earth," Nachau explained.

Kanem adjusted himself on the seat to listen more.

"The purpose of life is to glorify God," Nachau disclosed.

"I am hearing this for the first time in my life."

"But do you understand what I said?"

"It sounds good, but I am still confused."

"What is it?"

"I have been in the village trying to be somebody important, but all my efforts failed. Eventually, my own people banished me from the village. Does God really care for me?"

Nachau smiled at Kanem's ignorance, and continued to teach him in order to clarify his thinking. "Someone shared a story of a city of lepers, where nobody was allowed to go in, and come back to a normal society. The lepers were left to survive on their own. Out of pity, a priest, who was moved by the poor condition of the lepers decided to go, and stay with them against all odds. Eventually, he became infected and died, but he was able by God's grace to make a tremendous impact on the lives of the people," Nachau narrated.

Kanem looked on with interest.

"Do you think God loves what this man did?" Nachau asked.

"Sure! Everybody would be happy with what the man did."

"It is not about comfort or pain; but about God using us to bless the lives of others," Nachau emphasized.

"I don't want to be a blessing to my village. The only thing the people deserve is the pain of my anger. They will surely pay one day for what they did to me and my mother," Kanem said angrily.

"A community hardly initiates evil against one person. They often react to something. Can you tell me why they banished you?" Nachau curiously asked.

"I don't want to talk about it," Kanem reacted quickly.

"You reduce the weight of your burden when you share it with someone. You don't have to let the tears in your eyes become permanent, because they can distort your true view of the future," Nachau encouraged.

"Sometimes I feel like committing suicide. Life is really miserable!" Kanem lamented.

"I can tell you the easiest way to commit suicide if you want to," Nachau jokingly said.

Kanem forced himself to smile.

"Only cowards commit suicide. Frustration means overflow. It is a good tool for removing dirt from our lives."

"What do you mean?"

"Rejection adds value to acceptance. You will value the gift of sight more after you have been cured of blindness."

Kanem smiled, as he appreciated Nachau's insight.

"You have not yet told me why they sent you out of the village," Nachau insisted to know.

"They said that I was a terror to the village."

Nachau smiled at the disclosure of Kanem.

"Why did you smile?"

"I am just wondering how a young man like you can be a terror to a whole village," Nachau replied jokingly.

Kanem also smiled. "It is because you don't know what I can do."

"Are your father and mother alive?" Nachau asked.

"My father is dead," Kanem replied. "But why did you ask?"

"How did your father live before he died?"

"I think you are now going very far."

"Sometimes long journeys are needed for right solutions to be found," Nachau explained.

"He was the most useless father I have ever known!" Kanem reacted.

"Was he also a terror to the village?"

"Not just to the village, but also to his family," Kanem replied.

"It is easier for a person to make a major decision than for a whole community to do so. Your village only reacted to what your father started."

"You mean my father was directly responsible for what had happened to me?" Kanem curiously asked.

"Your father chose to live the way he did. You have the opportunity to live better. What happened to you was your choice. A dry leaf under a tree is a warning to the green ones."

"I will never forgive my father for what he did to us," Kanem said angrily.

"How will your bitterness against your father affect him now that he is dead?"

Kanem kept quiet.

"Forgiveness releases you from bondage. It balances you well for the potential development in you."

"What is the meaning of potential?" Kanem asked, after thinking for awhile.

"I am glad you asked this question."

Kanem smiled in expectation.

"The invisible teeth of an infant are like the hidden potential in a person, waiting for the right time to show themselves," Nachau explained.

"What do you mean?"

"It means that within each of us lies something great that we can use by God's grace to change our world. Once it is utilized well, we would discover that one potential leads to another."

"Does that involve all of us?" Kanem asked.

"Yes."

"I doubt my involvement."

"Why did you say that?"

"I failed in everything I tried to do!"

"A question was asked, 'How did water enter into the coconut?'"

"I don't know how," Kanem replied with a smile.

"Think about it. Just like the coconut, there are also sweet potential in all of us that can only be reached when we discover what we are in this world for," Nachau explained.

"Is that the same as vision?"

"No. A vision is different. It is the ability to see problems from a solution-oriented perspective. For instance, if you see people getting involved in drug addiction, and also see how you can help them stop, that is vision."

*

After a few hours into the journey, the bus stopped in Gombe State, where some passengers were waiting to board at the bus company's branch office.

The moment the bus door opened, most of the passengers alighted to ease themselves, and to get something to drink and eat. Nachau too alighted along with Kanem.

Kanem moved away from Nachau, bought a cigarette, lit it and started smoking. Nachau became concerned when he saw him. He moved closer to him.

"Why do you smoke?"

"I just like smoking," Kanem reluctantly replied.

"Every smoker smokes for a reason. To like smoking is only an excuse used for shortcut explanation."

"It makes me feel good whenever I need to escape from the pressure of my problems."

"Do your problems return after what you called 'escape?'"

"I don't understand what you mean."

"I am sure you do," Nachau said with a smile.

Kanem also smiled. "The more the pressure on me, the more I smoke."

"Overcoming problems is better than ignoring them. The more you ignore them, the more they possess you."

Kanem listened attentively.

"When did you start smoking?"

"Two years ago," Kanem replied reluctantly.

"How much do you spend daily?" Nachau further asked.

"A minimum of one hundred Naira."

"Spending a minimum of one hundred Naira a day for two years means you have spent seventy-three thousand Naira on cigarettes," Nachau explained after calculating with his cell phone.

Kanem was surprised on hearing that.

"Have you not cheated yourself?" Nachau asked.

Kanem remained silent sensing the truth in Nachau's analysis.

"You should now imagine how far you would have gone in your potential development assuming that you had invested this amount of money well," Nachau explained.

With this news, Kanem could not continue smoking. He discarded the half stick of cigarette in his hand. "I have never thought of it in this way."

"It is cheaper to be good than to be reckless with your life," Nachau emphasized.

Kanem nodded in agreement.

As the conductor was loading some luggage in the boot of the bus, a passenger complained that he was squeezing his luggage. Instead of the conductor apologizing, he harshly spoke to the passenger. As a result, they started exchanging nasty words against each other, which led to a fight.

Nachau, in company of others, intervened to settle the fight. The problem was resolved, and the conductor apportioned more blame for being careless.

The driver called the conductor aside to warn him not to endanger the company's image by any repetition of his actions.

The driver later entered the bus, and blew the horn. A woman carrying a baby struggled to enter the bus. Kanem, who was standing close to her, helped her by carrying the baby so that she could enter easily.

"Thank you," the woman said.

"You are welcome," Kanem replied, as he handed over the baby to her after she was settled in her seat.

CHAPTER 2

Nachau deliberately avoided talking to Kanem to allow him to think over the lessons he had taught him, and to test whether he had genuinely developed an interest in the conversation.

Kanem struggled within himself trying to decide whether to ask a question or not. He didn't want to unnecessarily disturb Nachau.

"Sir?"

"Yes," Nachau replied calmly.

"I have a question. I hope I will not disturb you?"

"Not at all. Please, ask," Nachau replied in anticipation.

"How do I identify my potential?"

"Asking this question shows that you have already started."

"How?" Kanem asked in confusion.

"You asked because you have started thinking. All you need is a confirmation from me that what you have been wishing to be is really what I was talking about. I am the one to ask you a question."

Kanem looked at Nachau with interest.

"What do you want to be?" Nachau asked.

"It has been my ambition to be a medical doctor."

"Do you still nurse this ambition?"

"I can't tell now."

"How do you feel whenever you see a doctor or sick person?"

"It makes me feel like becoming a doctor. A sick person makes me feel I should help him or her."

"Potential makes you a captive once you discover it. It creates an unquenchable burden that can only be overcome through its realization," Nachau explained.

"You are right. I often feel a great burden for medicine like the one you described."

"That burden should lead you to action," Nachau emphasized.

"I really need to know how I can start," Kanem desperately asked.

"There was a time I removed some flowers from my flower pots, and threw them away. A goat came, sniffed the flowers, and moved away without eating any. The second goat also came, and sniffed the flowers. However, the third goat came, sniffed, and started eating the flowers. One of the goats which had refused to eat came back, and joined the third goat in eating the flowers," Nachau narrated.

Kanem looked on in expectation.

"What do you think made the third goat eat the flowers?" Nachau asked.

"Courage. It took the risk that the rest were not at first willing to take," Kanem answered.

"You got it right," Nachau responded happily.

"You mean without courage to begin with, there is no way I can use my potential?"

"Courage fuels determination," Nachau replied.

"It sounds very easy, but in reality it seems like chasing the wind."

"With the right vision, it is possible to chase the wind and cage it," Nachau replied with a smile while imagining the struggles in Kanem's mind.

Kanem too smiled. "It is true. You have answers for everything."

"You also have the right seed- questions that make right answers possible," Nachau jokingly remarked.

The conductor interrupted their conversation by asking them to show their booking tickets for confirmation. It was their normal routine of checking whether there were illegal passengers on the bus and to find out that all passengers were seated in their rightful seats.

Having checked their tickets, the bus conductor returned the tickets to each of them, and moved to other passengers.

Nachau removed two cans of juice from his bag and gave one to Kanem.

"Thank you," Kanem said after collecting the juice.

"You are always welcome."

"I hope I am not a burden to you?" Kanem gently asked.

"There is a purpose for our meeting today. A moment with you in this bus did not take God by surprise," Nachau replied. "You are a blessing, Kanem, not a burden," he emphasized.

"I am grateful for your kindness," Kanem said.

As they sipped the juice, an announcement in the bus, made by a young man who was well dressed in a suit got their attention. He claimed to be a pastor, whose ministry was to share the Word of God with people in buses. He asked all the people to pray. Nachau and Kanem stopped sipping the juice, and closed their eyes to pray. The prayer took some time. After that, the pastor got people involved in singing songs of praise to God.

He delivered a sermon on the need for people to repent from their sins and obtain eternal life. At the end of the sermon, he passed round a small bag for people to give offerings as their support to the work of evangelism. Some responded positively, while others did not.

The driver of the bus took a sharp corner as soon as they reached Bauchi, the next State after Gombe from Yola. On reaching their branch office, the driver pulled up right in front of the booking office, where passengers who had booked in Bauchi were waiting eagerly to be conveyed to Lagos.

The preacher thanked the people for listening and for their support and alighted. Most of the passengers also came down feeling relieved from the stress of the journey.

Kanem went and bought two sachet of water, popularly known as 'pure water,' which cost ten naira, and gave one to Nachau.

"Thank you," Nachau stated.

"You are always welcome."

"You are a funny boy," Nachau remarked with a smile. "Excuse me please, let me go and ease myself," he added.

"I will sit here," Kanem said, as he pointed at a chair under a tree.

Kanem thought over their discussions, wondering whether the ideas Nachau had shared with him were worth trying out. He tried to figure out how he could start doing something that would help him achieve the purpose of life. He did not know when the passengers started getting on the bus.

Having entered the bus, Kanem met a passenger who came from Bauchi wrongly seated on his seat. He demanded that the passenger vacate the seat, but he refused. As a result, they started a noisy quarrel.

When the attention of the conductor was drawn to the problem, it was discovered a mistake was made in issuing out tickets. Kanem had the same seat number as the other passenger.

In the heat of the quarrel, Nachau suddenly came in. When Kanem informed him of the problem, he convinced the other passenger to look for another seat since Kanem had been using the seat right from Yola. Nachau's suggestion received the support of the conductor of the bus, and some of the passengers. Eventually, Kanem was able to secure his seat again.

"It is really difficult to handle human beings!" Kanem said angrily.

"I agree with you. But it is possible," Nachau responded.

Kanem looked at Nachau expectantly.

"There is a saying that 'human beings are like bees. They are sweet, and also dangerous, depending on how you view them.' There is no way you can achieve the potential in you alone. You need the right people to help you do that; but the moment you begin to see them as you described, the more you may dig out gold, and throw it into a dustbin without knowing," Nachau explained.

"What do you mean by right people?"

"Before I share that with you, I will tell you something first. Can you remind me where exactly we stopped in our last discussion in the bus before we were interrupted?"

"You told me that I am a blessing, not a burden."

"I am glad you still remember that."

Kanem smiled.

"When you are convinced about what God wants you to do, you don't need to rush into it without preparation. It is very important that you depend on God to give you the manual," Nachau stated.

"Is the manual the same as the one that comes with a new radio?" Kanem asked curiously.

"Something like that. Always take the time to write out the vision anytime you have an insight on your assignment. This helps you not to forget the idea, so that you can communicate the vision effectively. People will take you seriously, when they see your ideas on paper," Nachau explained.

Kanem nodded in understanding.

"Do you love writing?"

"No."

"No wonder you have not jotted down all that we have been discussing."

Kanem laughed. "I don't have a pen and paper," he tried to excuse his lack of interest in writing.

"You did not ask," Nachau said, as he removed a pen from his pocket and a jotter from his bag giving them both to Kanem.

"Thank you, sir," Kanem collected the items with a smile.

"During the preparation, God will shape you into the person He wants you to be. That is why somebody says that 'God will never use a person He has not trained,'" Nachau said.

Kanem wrote down the points quickly, as he tried to concentrate on getting more.

"Let us now look at the right people in your life. A rat one day told her parents that she had found someone to marry. When the parents inquired further, she informed them that it was a cat. That came to the parents as a surprise. They reminded her of the nature of cats. She insisted that her fiancé was a born-again cat, who had stopped eating rats."

This naive response made Kanem burst into laughter. "So what happened?" he curiously asked.

"The parents invited and interviewed the cat. Truly, they discovered that the repentance of the cat was genuine. On the wedding day, something terrible happened. Five of the rat's relatives went missing right in the Church building. It was not the groom, who had eaten them up, but his unrepentant friends and relatives attending the wedding. If that could happen inside the Church building, I wonder what would happen during the reception party." Nachau concluded.

Kanem laughed to the point of tears rolling down his cheeks. Some passengers turned to his direction to see what was happening. A man who sat behind them also laughed at the story.

Nachau smiled, as he waited for Kanem to finish laughing. "We all need the right people in life to help us achieve our assignments, not the people who will destroy us. You must have the courage to part with some people before you can stay focused," Nachau explained.

Kanem drank some water as he happily wrote some points. He opened the window wider, and threw the remaining water in a sachet out of the bus. Unknown to him, the wind took some water to a window some rows behind them. The water splashed on a passenger who alerted him rudely.

"But it wasn't my fault. It was the wind that took the water to your window!"Kanem replied rudely.

"It was your fault, Kanem," Nachau calmly said.

"I am sorry," Kanem apologized with a smile after thinking for a while.

"No problem," the man that complained said.

"Your value increases when you apologize for doing wrong," Nachau emphasized. "Let us look at the next point. You also need to wait for the right time. A pregnant woman does not expect a baby after two months of conception. A proverb pointed that a ripe mango does not need you to pluck it; on its own it will fall down for you to pick. Many people have caused problems for themselves simply because they are often in a hurry to accomplish the potential in them."

"Sir, what if the mango becomes rotten in the tree or eaten by birds before it falls down?" Kanem curiously asked.

"What do you think is the answer?"

Kanem laughed. "I don't know. That is why I asked."

"They may eat the mango, but they may not eat the seed. Take the seed, and plant it again," Nachau replied.

"But one may not be alive long enough to wait for the tree to grow, and eat from it," Kanem said.

"In that case, maybe your assignment is only to plant so that others will eat from it."

"You are scaring me with your knowledge, sir," Kanem stated.

"A proverb says that 'anybody who climbs trees with his teeth knows the trees that are bitter.'"

"There you go again," Kanem jokingly responded.

"We will continue with the conversation later. Let me rest," Nachau said with a smile.

"Thank you for your time. Today is the best day of my life," Kanem stated.

"I can only believe you when you put these principles into action," Nachau remarked.

Kanem laughed as he wrote down the points.

CHAPTER 3

The journey proceeded after conveying some passengers from Jos, Plateau State. Many passengers complained of the cold weather in Jos.

A few hours later most of the passengers were asleep because it was already night. Kanem could not sleep. The direction of his life was taking a new shape. He opened a blank new page of his jotter, and started writing down some ideas on how he would become a medical doctor, and achieve his potential. He believed that when he became a medical doctor, he would be able to help the people in his village. They wouldn't have to trek long distances before getting medical attention.

The bitterness in his heart had suddenly changed to compassion. He was beginning to feel great relief. For the first time in his life, he felt truly alive.

Suddenly, a man seated behind him touched him on the shoulder. Kanem curiously turned to him.

"This man makes a long journey short," the man said, pointing a hand towards Nachau.

"I often forget hours have passed by on our journey in company with him," Kanem responded.

As they were discussing, the bus suddenly pulled up. They had already reached Lokoja, in Kogi State.

Nachau woke up from sleep wondering why the bus had stopped. He expressed relief when he realized where they were.

"Why did we stop?" Kanem asked curiously.

"To eat and regain energy," Nachau replied, as he got ready to leave the bus. "Let's go out and eat."

"I am not hungry," Kanem said, trying to avoid being a burden to Nachau, because he did not have money for food on him.

"Everybody is hungry at this point. People that say they are not hungry often do not have money for food," Nachau explained.

Kanem smiled shyly.

"Correct me if I am wrong. Do you have money for food?"

"You are right, sir," Kanem admitted.

They went out to a restaurant and sat to eat. Each ordered for his choice food.

"I must admit that this journey is a school to me. I really appreciate your kindness," Kanem said.

"Thank God, don't thank me. I wouldn't have been speaking if nobody had been listening," Nachau replied.

"I know this is not the right time for a discussion, but anxiety will not allow me rest."

"Until you reach a point where you are driven by curiosity, you cannot effectively develop your potential. I am at your service. Every time is a good time," Nachau remarked.

"I have already started putting some ideas down on what I believe is the assignment of my life."

"Do you feel as if you have spent the past years for nothing?"

"How did you know that?" Kanem asked in surprise.

"That is what your potential makes you feel the moment you discover it," Nachau explained.

Kanem looked on in silence, wondering what kind of person Nachau was. "How can he know so much about life like this? Is he an angel sent by God to help me?" Kanem thought within himself.

"You may be thinking of why I know so much. Don't let that disturb you," Nachau said.

Kanem looked at Nachau keenly in amazement. Once again, he had read his mind.

"One day, if you continue achieving your potential, you will know that life is a chain reaction. Nothing is really new under the sun."

"My main problem is my inability to finish any project I start. I easily give up along the way. What can I do to overcome that?" Kanem asked.

"It's as if you read my mind. The next thing I want to discuss with you is perseverance. A friend told me a story of 'an old donkey that fell into a dry well, and cried for rescue. When the owner of the donkey was informed, he ordered that the donkey be buried alive in the well since both the donkey and the well were of little value to him."

Kanem listened attentively.

"As the donkey was waiting to be rescued, it suddenly started feeling some sand being dropped on its body. The donkey knew that it was not a rescue operation, but a burial. Instead of allowing itself to be buried, it started shaking off the sand until it eventually became a stepping ground for it to leap out of the well.'"

Kanem smiled as usual. "The donkey used its challenges to its advantage."

"That is the point. You should never allow anything to discourage you from achieving your potential. Perseverance is the confirmation that the vision you carry is still alive," Nachau explained.

Kanem quickly wrote down some points in his jotter.

"Learn to depend on God for the strength to carry on the task He has given you to the end; because the end of a matter is better than the beginning," Nachau said.

The waiter interrupted their discussions by serving the food they had ordered. As Nachau got ready to eat, Kanem was busy writing, as he ignored the food.

"Kanem, now is the time to eat. Writing can come later."

"I need to finish writing down some points first," Kanem replied.

Nachau responded with a laugh, as he began eating his food.

Kanem's attention was drawn to Nachau's laughter. "Why are you laughing, sir?" Kanem asked anxiously.

"It is of joy not of mockery."

Kanem stopped writing, and concentrated on Nachau.

"Potential becomes food, once it is awakened from sleep."

Kanem quickly wrote down the point in anticipation for more.

"Many people cheat, and kill only to have food on their tables. For you to have it, and ignore it is a sign that you have discovered something worthwhile."

Kanem was glued to his pen and jotter. "I feel like a prisoner of ideas."

"Then you must let ideas sentence you to life in prison," Nachau jokingly said.

"So it is better to be a prisoner of ideas than to live in the freedom of ignorance?" Kanem asked.

Nachau smiled, as he continued to eat.

Without any further word from Nachau, Kanem understood the answer to his question. As soon as he finished writing, he put the pen, and the jotter aside, and ate his food.

After eating, they suddenly heard people shouting outside. A thief, who was trying to steal a bag from a bus, had been caught.

The thief was crying, and begging the people for mercy; but nobody was willing to let him go. He was beaten to unconsciousness. The police on patrol came, and took him away from the crowd to the hospital.

Nachau and Kanem moved out of the restaurant into the rowdy crowd. Many people were busy discussing about the situation, while others were selling, and buying things.

A girl came to Nachau with smoked fish to buy. He told her that he had no need of the fish. The girl persisted, until he finally had no option, but to buy the fish. He gave it to Kanem for his own use.

From what the girl did, Kanem learnt a practical lesson on the value of persistence. The truth of knowledge as a chain reaction was vividly staring him in the face. He then knew that the era of his habit of abandoning projects was over.

When the driver entered the bus, and blew the horn, the passengers rushed in. The driver told the conductor to allow extra passengers to board. They call them 'Attachments.' They pay less to either keep standing in the bus, or sit on wooden chairs placed in the centre passage space of the bus. They often inconvenience the rightful passengers.

A passenger looked for his wife, but did not see her. He begged the driver to wait further, but the driver was in a hurry. Some passengers begged the driver to wait for the woman, while others were insulting her for causing a delay. Reluctantly, the driver waited. The man went out and searched for his wife. Eventually, he met her buying smoked fish. He became angry with her, and shouted at her. When they finally entered the bus, most of the passengers also shouted at her for her carelessness.

As they were getting ready to start the trip, the driver received a phone call from a friend, who was also a driver, advising him to remain where they were, because armed robbers were robbing people on the road not far away from their location.

The driver instructed the conductor to inform the passengers about the situation on ground. Fear gripped most of the passengers after the announcement.

The woman, who had earlier caused the delay, seized the opportunity to react against the passengers who had shouted at her. "All those who blamed me for the delay have to apologize, because of the blessing brought by the delay!"

Some of the passengers looked at her quietly, as her husband tried to stop her from further action. Eventually, after much persuasion, the husband prevailed on her to be quiet.

Nachau saw the blessing of the delay as an opportunity to share another lesson with Kanem.

"What have you learnt from what just happened?"

"I can't really figure out any special lesson from it," Kanem replied.

"Think very well, there is a lesson to be learnt from everything," Nachau encouraged.

"I remember the saying, 'every disappointment is a blessing,'" Kanem stated.

"You got it right, Kanem! You should always remember whenever you find yourself in any situation that God is always in control. He supplies all our needs."

"Talking about my needs, how can I get help from people to fund my project when I begin working to achieve my potential?"

"Your help comes from God. You must have faith in God before you can perform wonders," Nachau remarked.

"I often hear people complain of lack of support for worthwhile assignments."

"Every vision at first is like a foreign language. People need to understand it before participating actively in it," Nachau explained.

"Please, sir," the gentleman from behind interrupted their discussions politely. "My name is Calvin. I have been listening to your discussions for some hours. I hope you will not mind if I ask you a question?"

"Please, feel free to join us," Nachau replied.

"He talked to me about you when you were asleep," Kanem said, supporting Calvin's interest in the discussions.

"I heard everything you said," Nachau stated with a smile.

Kanem and Calvin also smiled.

"I am a graduate. I read business administration. For five years, I have been looking for a good job without success. As I am talking to you now, I think I am the most frustrated person in the world," Calvin lamented.

Nachau listened with keen interest. He deliberately kept quiet for a while after Calvin's explanation.

Calvin waited anxiously for the encouragement he knew Nachau was capable of giving.

"Mr. frustrated man in the world," Nachau addressed Calvin, as he broke the moment of silence.

Calvin and Kanem laughed.

"In all your efforts to look for a good job, have you ever thought of initiating a good one?" Nachau asked.

"Sometimes I thought of that, but whenever I looked at my poor background, and what people would say if I fail, I lack the courage to venture into any good project," Calvin explained.

"Calvin, no one with a dream is unemployed. There is a potential in you that wants to employ you. The more you spend time looking for employment somewhere, the more you render that potential dormant. I am happy you brought that up, because it shows that you are on your way to freedom."

Calvin and Kanem nodded in agreement.

"I also want you to know that you are not the most frustrated person in the world, you are only one of them," Nachau emphasized.

Calvin smiled as he listened with keen interest.

"Have you ever heard the proverb that 'no matter how far your village is, there is another village ahead?'" Nachau asked.

Both Calvin and Kanem said "No" as they laughed over the proverb. Nachau too joined them with a smile.

"True happiness doesn't depend on material things. It is the state of your mind. One day, in a discussion, somebody mentioned something that caught my attention. When he was a child, he had no material things, yet he was happy. That shows that once your way of thinking is right, you too will thank God even in a moment like this," Nachau explained.

"But is it really possible for someone to start something great without money?" Calvin asked.

"An idea attracts money. Sow a seed of a good idea, and see what happens next," Nachau replied.

"Sir," Kanem interrupted. "Calvin said something very important about failure, and people's response to those who tried, and failed. I think that is also an issue."

"The determination of a conqueror is fuelled by injuries. Failure is like a bus stop for more passengers, not the ultimate destination. God may allow you to be in tears, but not in shame," Nachau responded.

"I hate failure," Calvin said.

"Failure is a teacher. It washes your hands well so that you can handle success without stain," Nachau encouraged.

"Sir, are you sure all failures do that," Calvin asked curiously.

"All can, but not all will," Nachau replied.

"What do you mean, sir?" Calvin inquired further.

"They will if you accept them as opportunities to learn, and grow; but they cannot, if you don't," Nachau explained.

Suddenly, a man started calling on the driver to stop. He had a stomach-ache. He needed to go out of the bus to a nearby bush to ease himself. The driver refused to pay attention to the man's request. He kept on driving, contemplating the risk of pulling up on the outskirts.

Other passengers seated close to the man also joined in pleading.

Most of the passengers, who were asleep, woke up in fear, trying to find out what was happening.

The man could not bear the perpetual neglect of the driver to his request. He stood up from his seat, and moved closer to the driver's cabin, shouting at the driver to stop.

Nearing a town, the driver stopped the bus, and grumbled because of the delay that the stop would cause the journey.

The man ran out of the bus into the bush, unmindful of the risk of poisonous snakes. Many other passengers also used the opportunity to ease themselves.

After some minutes, the driver kept on blowing the horn, alerting the passengers who had disembarked, to enter the bus.

The man who had the problem came out of the bush relieved, and abused the driver for embarrassing him.

The driver and the conductor also responded to the man in like manner, threatening not to stop for anyone again until they reach the town where they would refuel.

Upon sitting down, the sick man asked loudly if anybody had a drug for him to take, because he knew that some people travel with drugs for first-aid purposes.

A woman removed some tablets from her bag, and asked him to come over to her seat, and collect them.

Without wasting much time, he rushed to her, and collected them. She also gave him some water to swallow the tablets. He thanked her for her kindness.

"There are some lessons in what just happened," Nachau said, as soon as calmness returned to the bus.

"What lessons, sir?" Calvin anxiously asked.

"I have already figured one out," Kanem said.

"We are listening," Nachau stated.

"Once you carry the burden of something, you have no rest until you accomplish what is required," Kanem disclosed.

"You got the first lesson right. You are beginning to scare me with your understanding," Nachau jokingly said.

"I am only responding to your treatments," Kanem said with a smile.

"What about other lessons?" Nachau asked.

"I cannot figure that out," Kanem replied.

"Never say you can't. It is better you say you have no idea about it."

"Okay," Kanem admitted.

"A person of vision does not mind what people will say against him when he is driven by the passion to deliver his potential," Nachau explained.

Calvin nodded in understanding.

"Many passengers were also pressed, but they did not have the courage to speak out. They only took the step forward after someone had taken the first risk. In the same way, you can make a great impact on the world by God's grace if you take the risk to convert ideas to projects. You can also misdirect if you don't," Nachau emphasized.

Nachau's explanations sank deep into the hearts of Kanem and Calvin. The calmness on their faces showed it all.

"It is really a great privilege meeting you, sir," Calvin calmly said.

"The privilege is mine. All for the glory of God," Nachau remarked.

Kanem looked on in deep appreciation of Nachau's wealth of wisdom, and his eagerness to share with them.

As they travelled through the night, Nachau jokingly said, "No matter the significance of a person's vision, it is important to know when to work, and when to rest. Now my time for rest has come. You also need to sleep."

"I can't sleep. I am feeling as if I am in a battlefield of thoughts," Kanem said.

"You are going through an expansion. Ideas make soft pillows rough. The more you try to sleep, the more they keep you awake. Sometimes sleepless nights are assets," Nachau explained.

Kanem and Calvin smiled in understanding.

Calvin also got involved in thinking over what Nachau had taught them. He was also committed to allowing ideas to keep him awake.

Gradually, most of the passengers were deep asleep. As they fell silent, the movement of the bus through the deep darkness could be heard.

A passenger next to a nursing mother was disturbing her with his irritating snores. She could hardly sleep because of that. She tapped him gently on the shoulder to adjust his sleeping position to help stop the snoring, but that did not work.

Her baby woke up due to her constant movement and started crying, desiring milk. As the mother drew the mouth of the baby to the breast, her attention was also on the snoring man.

Continually, she kept on tapping the man's shoulder until he woke up from sleep.

She asked him to control his snoring. He looked at her angrily, and went back to sleep, snoring worse than before.

Out of anger, the woman tapped him again. Furiously, he warned her not to touch him again; but she remained committed in making sure he stops. As the quarrel progressed, the baby forsook the mother's breast, and cried louder. The woman's attention shifted completely to the baby, ignoring the man.

The man could not sleep anymore. He switched on the light; picking a book from his bag, he began to read it.

After a while, the baby became calm, and began to sleep.

CHAPTER 4

Nachau woke up to read. When he switched on the light, he saw Kanem, lost in deep thought. "You are still thinking?"

"Yes, sir," Kanem replied calmly.

"I hope you are not thinking of the attachments of life?"

Kanem smiled. "What do you mean by attachments of life?"

Their conversation made Calvin wake up. He did not want to miss any part of it.

"The attachments the bus is carrying," Nachau said, pointing at the extra passengers on board, "Are more than the capacity of the bus. They are gaining today, but losing tomorrow."

Kanem and Calvin once again listened attentively.

"So also is life. Sometimes we try to force ourselves beyond what we can afford. This leads to worries over many things, and at the end, loss of focus replaces the impact of our potential. You need self-discipline first, before you can encourage change in others. We must learn to deal with issues in our lives that take us away from our visions."

"Can you help us recognise what some of those attachments are?" Calvin asked.

"Fear is one of them," Nachau replied. "Many great ideas have been assassinated by fear. As a result, we have more wishers than doers."

"I was one of the wishers," Kanem quickly stated.

"Why did you use past tense?" Nachau inquired.

"I now belong to the doers," Kanem replied.

"Good to hear that. I hope to see greater results one day," Nachau responded.

"I now also belong to the doers," Calvin said.

"A proverb says that 'running away from your fear is more painful than facing it,'" Nachau emphasized.

Kanem and Calvin nodded, acknowledging acceptance.

"You must also be careful with the temptation of sexual immorality. A potential in action attracts the opposite sex," Nachau stated. "Do you have a female friend?" he asked Kanem.

Kanem smiled shyly. "I used to have, but I don't know if she still cares."

"But do you care for her?" Nachau asked further.

"I don't know."

"I am still waiting for the right answer."

"Yes, I still do," Kanem admitted.

"What about you Calvin?"

"I do."

"Avoiding a reckless lifestyle shows how much you cherish the potential in you," Nachau explained.

"You mean it is possible to live without a sexual relationship?" Kanem inquired.

"Is it not?" Nachau asked.

"There is a saying that 'the human body is not wood,'" Calvin replied with a smile.

"That means what?" Nachau asked, also with a smile.

"You know what I meant, sir," Calvin replied jokingly.

"A minister shared a story of a young man, who was involved in a sexual relationship with a girl against his wishes. Anytime he informed her of his intention to quit, the girl responded by fainting. As a result, the boy felt trapped. One day, he shared his burden with a pastor, who advised him to quit the relationship, and not be afraid if the girl fainted. When he tried it, she fainted as usual. He waited for her to recover without changing his mind."

Kanem and Calvin laughed.

"It was really a funny way to freedom," Kanem said.

"There is a switch attached to everybody. Self-control is impossible if you try to be in charge of yours, but possible by God's grace," Nachau emphasized.

"Sir, the problem is with many girls nowadays. They often harass us sexually with the way they dress, and it is not easy for me to have self-control. I don't want my female friend to think I am not normal," Calvin responded.

"Do you have a sister?" Nachau inquired.

"Yes," Calvin answered.

"Would you feel sexually harassed if you saw your sister naked?" Nachau asked.

"No," Calvin quickly replied.

"What about you Kanem?"

"A normal person should not be sexually harassed by his sister's nakedness," Kanem replied.

"Why?" Nachau asked.

"She is my sister," Calvin answered quickly.

"Does being your sister make her nakedness different from other girls that you claim are harassing you?" Nachau inquired.

"They all carry the same features," Calvin replied calmly.

"Your way of thinking is very important in overcoming sexual temptation. If you have good intentions in relating with other girls, like those that you have towards your sister, you will not allow yourself to be carried away by their harassments. What God thinks about you is the most important thing in life."

"To be honest, it is not easy to do that, sir," Kanem stated.

"I agree with you. But it can be done by God's grace," Nachau said.

Calvin and Kanem kept quiet, thinking deeply about the discussion.

"Another attachment you must drop is laziness. You have to conquer the influence of your bed on you. What you have not done cannot do itself. The word 'later' is an enemy of 'now.' Every time should be the right time for you to do something good. One word on a paper is better than a plain sheet of paper," Nachau explained.

Kanem and Calvin still listened attentively.

"Kanem, I observed that you have stopped writing for a while," Nachau said.

"There is no light, and I don't know how to switch it on," Kanem stated, as he tried to defend himself.

"Why didn't you ask?" Nachau inquired.

Kanem smiled.

"You were afraid people would see you as a village boy?" Nachau asked jokingly.

Kanem nodded in approval of what Nachau said.

"All of us were born weak, and helpless. It is through learning that we become strong. You must always have the humility to ask when you are not sure," Nachau encouraged, as he raised his hand to switch on the light situated above Kanem.

"Thank you," Kanem said.

Nachau smiled. "The next attachment is unhealthy competition. Many people measure success by what others do. Each of us has his own style, and timing for dream actualization. The more you move with the speed of others, the more you sink, because life is sinkable in nature," Nachau explained.

"But what about if the other person is doing the same thing with me? Is it not good to compare to see whether I am making progress or not?" Calvin curiously asked.

"You can learn from everybody, but don't compare. Success is not measured by speed, but in your ability to commit to a project. How would you know whether the person you compare yourself with is moving towards the right direction?"

Kanem took some time to write the points down.

"Selfishness is also another attachment. There is a temptation to use people only as tools to achieve your vision. You must always remember the saying that 'a strong man stands up for himself, but a stronger man stands up for others,'" Nachau stated.

At this point, Calvin picked his phone, and tried to make a call, but it was not getting through. Desperation and frustration were vivid on his face.

"You must always be focused. There is also the attachment of a busy lifestyle. You should not pursue your vision with other things, but you can do other things for your vision," Nachau continued, while concentrating on the sudden nervousness on Calvin's face.

Unexpectedly, the driver applied the brakes, and shouted "Armed robbers." They had fallen into a trap. The armed robbers had crossed the road with big stones. The driver tried to reverse immediately, but he quickly noticed two of the armed robbers beside the road holding guns. They shouted a warning to the driver to give up trying to escape, or they would shoot the tyres of the bus.

In fear, the driver stopped the bus. Some armed men came out of the jungle. They hit the door hard, and commanded the driver to open it. The passengers, who were asleep, woke up.

Fear gripped most of the passengers. Some were crying aloud, while others were trying to hide some parts of their money in different places.

The armed robbers rushed into the bus when the driver opened the door, and commanded the driver to switch on the main light.

One of the armed robbers started addressing the passengers as soon as the light came on. "We are here only for your money which will soon become ours. We won't harm anybody if you cooperate with us. Do you understand?"

The passengers only looked on nervously.

"Do you understand?" the armed robber repeated harshly.

Many of the passengers answered "Yes" in confusion.

One of the armed robbers moved to Calvin, removed a pistol, and gave it to him. "Boss, the operation is ready for your further command," the armed robber said.

The passengers gazed in disbelief. Nachau too, could not avoid being surprised.

Calvin gently stood up. He avoided eye contact with Nachau and Kanem, as he walked away from his seat to address his fellow passengers.

The moment he got to the front, he stood in silence for a while, looking directly at his fellow passengers.

"Boss, I hope you are okay? We are waiting for the next step," one of the armed robbers remarked, because he had never seen Calvin in such a mood during an operation. He knew him as a tough and merciless leader whenever he led such an operation.

"Ladies and gentlemen, my fellow passengers," Calvin broke the moment of confusion. "I entered this bus some hours ago for a time like this. My mission was to organize the operation from inside. That I did successfully," he explained. "Sir," he turned to Nachau. "The frustration I told you about led to this group. I am the initiator. All these people are my friends," he emphasized, pointing at the armed robbers.

"Boss, we are in the middle of an operation. There is no time for long speeches," one of the armed robbers cautioned.

Suddenly, another bus fell into the armed robbers' trap. The shouting outside became louder as the robbers tried to force the driver to stop the bus.

Luckily, the driver managed to reverse. He turned, and escaped amidst gunshots.

The gunshots instilled great fear in the minds of most of the passengers in the two buses.

Calvin commanded his men through the window to stop shooting. Immediately, they stopped the shootings.

"None of you should worry. We will take nothing of yours," Calvin disclosed calmly to his fellow passengers.

"What do you mean boss?" one of the armed robbers asked harshly. His name is Janbo.

"I have found another way for all of us; a better way that will make us real achievers."

"What other way?" Janbo asked curiously.

"I will explain to you later. Just trust me," Calvin replied.

Even with Calvin's announcement, the tension in the bus did not subside. The passengers did not believe him. Only a practical assurance would convince them. As long as the armed robbers were still in the bus, anything could happen.

"Sir," Calvin moved towards Nachau, still holding the gun. "Discussing with you has helped me discover the path of peace. I will never forget this trip. My generation will not be in sorrow because of me."

Out of surprise and joy, Nachau stood up, and confidently looked directly at Calvin. Shame did not allow Calvin to do the same.

Nachau held one of Calvin's hands in appreciation of what God had started doing in his life. "A question was asked, 'When a fish marries a bird, where would they live after the wedding?'"

Calvin thought for a while. "It is better they don't get married," he calmly answered.

"You also need to disengage from this type of lifestyle. You are created to glorify God. You are a great man Calvin. A better life awaits you," Nachau encouraged.

"Thank you for everything, sir," Calvin remarked.

"God loves you. No matter the wrongs you have done in the past, He can make things right for you if you ask Him to," Nachau said, as he removed a Holy Bible and one of his books from his bag, giving them to Calvin. "This is my complimentary card. Feel free to call me," Nachau added, as he gave Calvin the card.

They hugged each other. Calvin was in tears. The majority of the passengers looked on in confusion.

"Thank you too," Calvin said, as he turned to Kanem, and shook hands with him.

Calvin immediately picked his bag, rushed out of the bus with his friends, and joined the other armed robbers who were outside. After a few minutes of discussion, they ran into the jungle.

It took some time before normalcy was restored on the bus. Some of the passengers came to Nachau, and thanked him for his help even though they didn't understand what really had gone on between him and Calvin.

"All for the glory of God," Nachau repeatedly replied.

"I didn't know that Calvin was a useless man," Kanem said angrily.

"A useless man doesn't attack a bus and leave without robbing people of their possessions. Calvin was a great man who only made some mistakes in the past," Nachau remarked

"You are right. Anybody can make mistakes," Kanem admitted.

CHAPTER 5

When Nachau checked the time, it was 6:13 a.m. The driver drove into a service station to refuel.

Most of the passengers used the opportunity to ease themselves. When they got out of the bus, Nachau taught Kanem another lesson.

"People become so busy with their work that they often forget to retreat for personal enrichment. Just like this bus, refuelling is the trigger of continuity. Becoming better is your choice."

"The bus can stop on the way for lack of fuel assuming the driver refused to refuel," Kanem stated.

"Kanem, I really appreciate your sharp understanding," Nachau commended.

Kanem laughed in appreciation.

The passengers entered the bus after refuelling, and the journey continued.

"How do you retreat, sir?" Kanem curiously asked.

"I pray, read, and observe things," Nachau replied.

"I am sure you are a man of the people. How do you relate with them, and still have a retreat?"

"A friend once advised me that when running, I should never pay attention to those clapping for me, or against me, because they are all distractions. In view of that, I sometimes withdraw from the crowd in order to become better in relating with the crowd," Nachau replied.

Interrupting them, a woman shouted at the top of her voice, crying bitterly. The passengers close to her tried to calm her down, but she seemed to be beyond control. "My son! My son!" The woman shouted repeatedly.

A phone text had just informed her that she had lost her only son in an accident.

Eventually she fainted. The driver quickly stopped the bus in a nearby town so she could be treated properly. Some fellow passengers rushed her out of the bus, and two gallons of water poured onto her body. It took concerted efforts to revive her.

On recovery, the woman insisted on returning to Yola to be with her family. However, other passengers persuaded her to reach Lagos, where she would more easily board a bus back home.

There was silence when the passengers eventually returned to the bus.

"Sometimes I wonder why people die," Kanem broke the moment of silence.

"Death came into the world as a result of sin. As you pursue your potential, death plays the good and unique role of reminding you that you need to finish the task on time. You need not be lazy or procrastinate."

Kanem looked at Nachau calmly.

"That is why whatever you want to do; you should do it now, before it is too late. When a person accepts Jesus as his Lord and Saviour, he enjoys a wonderful relationship with Him, even after death."

Kanem still looked calm, but was obviously worried. "You told Calvin that God can make things right for him no matter the wrongs he had done in the past if he asks."

"Yes," Nachau responded.

"I really want God to make things right for me."

"Jesus came into the world to save us from the bondage of sin. He invites us to come to Him with all our burdens and He will give us rest," Nachau explained.

Kanem listened attentively.

"God loves you and He will be happy if you love Him too. You will benefit nothing if you gain the whole world and lose your soul. All you need to do is to confess your sins and accept Jesus as your Lord and Saviour," Nachau emphasized.

"I have done terrible things in the past. Would God really forgive me as you have described?"

"Do you remember yesterday, when I almost missed the bus?" Nachau asked.

Kanem nodded.

"The driver was considerate to stop and open the door for me to enter. Similarly, God is waiting patiently and willing to open the door of salvation for you to enter into a wonderful fellowship with Him," Nachau explained.

"I really want to accept Jesus as my Lord and Saviour," Kanem said calmly.

"Would you want to do it now?" Nachau asked.

"Yes."

Both of them held their hands, bowed their heads and prayed. Kanem asked Jesus to come into his heart. He kept quiet for a moment after the prayer, feeling a great awareness of a new journey of life.

"It is important you learn to constantly depend on God, read the Holy Bible, and pray for your spiritual growth. Having fellowship with the Church is also very important," Nachau explained carefully.

Tears rolled down Kanem's cheeks. He became nervous on the seat as if he had swallowed a burning charcoal.

"Why are you crying?" Nachau curiously asked.

Kanem looked at Nachau with the intention of explaining his situation, but couldn't explain why.

"I guess you have a visit from your past."

"Yes," Kanem remarked, still sobbing. "I am thinking of my father. I should have welcomed his invitation for reconciliation before he died!"

Nachau felt pity for him, because of the pain of realizing such an error. "That is a fact you have to live with. Count it as one of the errors you had made in the past. Don't make it a burden."

"I don't think I can forgive myself," Kanem said, as he thought more about how hard his father tried to see him and how his mother pleaded in tears for him to reconcile with his father. "My mother used to tell me that life is too short to be wasted on malice. A chance to forgive is more precious than gold."

"If you don't let it go, you will not make progress. Ignorance made soap reject the friendship of water. You blame yourself now because of the light you have discovered; or can you blame a blind man for living in darkness before he was healed of blindness?"

Kanem wiped away his tears with the collar of his shirt in response to Nachau's encouragement.

"Keep moving, my friend. There is a saying that 'it is easier to push a rolling car.' You must learn to motivate yourself; because motivation lubricates the machinery of progress," Nachau emphasized.

*

The passengers disembarking in Ibadan, Oyo State, expressed relief when they finally reached their destination. The driver pulled over at their branch office.

"Is this Lagos?" Kanem anxiously asked.

"No. This is Ibadan, in Oyo," Nachau answered.

When Nachau and Kanem moved out of the bus to relax, as if it was a dream, Kanem saw Pamale, the friend he would be staying with in Lagos. He rushed to him calling him by name to be sure he was the one.

When Pamale saw Kanem, he also ran to him. At a point, they met and hugged each other in excitement.

"What are you doing here? I thought you are supposed to be waiting for me in Lagos?" Kanem asked Pamale curiously.

"I really forgot that you were coming. Many things came up since you informed me of your coming. People who live in Lagos often need reminders," Pamale said.

"I am happy we met, before I reached Lagos, only to put up with disappointment," Kanem stated.

Pamale smiled. "I am happy to see you too. How is everything in the village?"

"People live in hope for better days to come. What are you doing here?"

"I was able to work hard and saved some money. I bought this small car," pointing at a car close to them. "I am on my way home to start a transport company," Pamale explained.

"That is a good idea. I am surprised to hear you talk like that, because you have been a master of reckless spending," Kanem said.

"People don't remain the same forever. I attended a seminar on 'Discovering the Purpose of Life.' There I learnt many things. We all have potential that we need to discover and achieve them for God's glory, so that we can positively impact the world," Pamale explained.

Kanem laughed, as he listened to Pamale. The transformation he had already seen in Pamale's life made him feel like he was getting to know him for the first time.

"Why are you laughing?" Pamale asked.

"I am laughing at both the transformation and the coincidence, because I also met a man, who taught me what you have just said. Let me introduce you to him."

The friends went to Nachau, who was standing alone, looking at the activities around the bus. Pamale surprisingly identified him as the speaker at the seminar he had told Kanem about.

"Sir, meet Pamale, the friend I was to stay with in Lagos," Kanem said, as he interrupted Nachau's concentration.

"Hello Pamale," Nachau greeted, as he shook hands with him.

"Good morning, sir," Pamale replied respectfully.

"How are you today?" Nachau asked.

"I am doing fine," Pamale answered.

"Did both of you plan to meet here?" Nachau inquired.

"No, it was a coincidence. He bought a car and he is on his way home to start a transport business," Kanem explained.

"He forgot you were coming?" Nachau asked.

"Yes, but it was my fault. I did not remind him," Kanem admitted.

"Sir, were you the speaker in a seminar at the Divine Vision Church, Ikeja, four months ago?" Pamale asked.

"Yes," Nachau quickly remembered.

"It is a pleasure meeting you, sir. I was one of the participants. My life changed after that seminar." Pamale took some time to explain some lessons he had learnt from the seminar and the steps he took to use them.

Nachau was full of happiness on hearing what Pamale said. "Knowledge is application. I am really glad I met you."

"I am glad too," Pamale responded.

"You seem to be everywhere, sir," Kanem stated jokingly.

"That is not correct. I am only trying to do the little I can do before sunset, when there will be no more time to work," Nachau replied with a smile.

Kanem and Pamale laughed.

"What do you hope to do now?" Nachau asked Kanem curiously.

Kanem kept quiet for a while, as he thought of what to do next. "I think there is no need for me to proceed to Lagos."

Nachau and Pamale listened.

"I am going back home with Pamale, to put to use what I now believe is my potential," Kanem disclosed.

"May I know what that is?" Nachau asked.

"By the grace of God, I will seek for admission to the university, study hard and become a medical doctor," Kanem replied.

"This statement is evidence that you have just been healed of blindness," Nachau remarked.

Kanem and Pamale smiled.

"How do you intend to solve the problem of the banishment?" Nachau asked.

"I was the problem, not the people. Since I am now better, I am sure the people of my village would also become better. My mother once told me that 'with a good approach, a young goat can suck a hyena's breast,'" Kanem answered.

"Your mother must be a wise woman," Nachau said.

"Now I believe she is," Kanem remarked.

"What banishment?" Pamale asked.

"I will explain everything to you on the way," Kanem replied.

"For you to achieve your assignment there must first of all be denial of self. The dying of a seed so that it can live again," Nachau encouraged.

"Thank you, sir, for everything," Kanem responded calmly.

"To God be the glory," Nachau said.

"Everything has to go based on a plan. I am a businessman. I only have unoccupied seats for two passengers in my car. I hope you have money to pay for your seat? No business should be done free, or else there will be no growth," Pamale informed Kanem.

Kanem looked surprised at such a disclosure. He thought Pamale would not mention that as a friend.

"You are really into business. That is why business people advocate that 'there will be growth in business, when friends and well-wishers pay for the services rendered,'" Nachau supported Pamale's business commitment.

"Well, in that case, I will look for money to pay you immediately we reach home," Kanem said.

"As a better alternative, I will myself pay your transport fare," Pamale stated jokingly.

Nachau and Kanem laughed at Pamale's statement, and commitment to his business.

"Let me go, and get my bag from the bus," Kanem said, as he rushed to the bus.

"That's okay," Nachau responded.

When Kanem returned after getting his bag, he thanked Nachau once again for all that God had used him to do in his life. "I will never forget you, sir," Kanem said.

"You are a blessing to our country and beyond. It is a privilege to know you now, before you become very busy," Nachau encouraged, as he hugged Kanem.

Both of them shed tears of joy. Nachau removed his complimentary card, and gave to Kanem.

The driver started the bus, getting ready to move. Nachau looked at the bus as the driver waited for the passengers to enter. Another great lesson flashed into his mind. "Kanem, God has ignited the potential in you the same way the bus driver ignited the bus. The driver has a choice to move forward, or remain in one place and waste the fuel."

"By God's grace, I will not waste the fuel," Kanem replied.

"There is also another way for the driver to waste the fuel," Nachau said.

"What way is that?" Pamale, who was listening to them with interest asked.

"Don't let the tank leak. Avoid anything that will not please God," Nachau explained.

Kanem and Pamale nodded in understanding.

"Someone shared a story of 'a mother fish and her little baby. One day, fishermen caught the little fish. As they were taking it away, the mother fish was crying, because she would miss her baby. The little fish looked at the mother, and encouraged her to remain hopeful until she sees smoke, because there was every possibility for it to come back alive,'" Nachau narrated.

Both Kanem and Pamale laughed over the story.

"Don't give up no matter what happens. Life is like a bus ride. There is a time to begin the ride, and a time to end it. In the interim is a chance to do something worthwhile," Nachau explained.

With this encouragement, the friends departed, each towards the path of his potential.

CHAPTER 6

Calvin eventually received Jesus as his Lord and Saviour. He went to a seminary and studied Missions and Evangelism. After graduation, he became a missionary, and started a ministry, preaching the Gospel, especially in rural areas. His gang members, apart from Janbo, also received Jesus, and joined him in the ministry.

Janbo formed his own gang. One day, during an operation on a bank, the police ambushed and killed all of them.

Kanem went back home and apologized to the elders, and people of the village. He also informed them of his new life. They accepted his apology and forgave him, with a warning that he should never be found disturbing the peace of the village again. His mother was very happy to have her son back in the village.

Kanem got admission to a university, and studied medicine. He eventually became a medical doctor and later a consultant in surgery, working, not only in his village, state, or country, but also internationally.

He eventually got married to Nina. God blessed them with three children. The first son was named Nachau.

Kanem also wrote a book. As part of the book's introduction, he wrote:

Every day of our lives, we have opportunities to choose how we want to live. These privileges exist only for a while. If we do not use them well, our stories will have unhappy endings. The sunrise represents the time you and I were born, and the sunset is the time we die; when all our potential goes down to silence in us. We can't plan or execute them ourselves.

Life is full of challenges to act well. Every opportunity we have is a chance to make things better.

I won't forget Nachau, a stranger, who became my friend, and now a mentor. To God be the glory.